Pieces of the Broken Jar

By: Chad Smith

Every word in this book was written by me. No AI was used for ideas or editing.
This comes from the heart.

To find more books by me visit:

www.gattaca.world

Copyright 2024

This collection is dedicated to Earl S. Braggs.

You inspired me with your passion. I learned more about writing in your classes than I can put into words. I'd like to think I would have brought any of these poems into your class, and a few of these...I did. I am sorry if I didn't learn enough.

"In which language do I keep silent?"

- Braggs, Earl, author. "In Which Language Do I Keep Silent.", by Anhinga Press, 2006.

"Time stands in the doorway
Peeling an apple.
It hurts here.
It hurts here."

- Jackson, Richard, author. "Alive All Day.", by Cleveland State University Poetry Center, 1992.

"I ponder the velocity of silence"

- Braggs, Earl, author. "In Which Language Do I Keep Silent.", by Anhinga Press, 2006.

"The whole world is a bottle
And life is but a dram
When the bottle gets empty
It sure ain't worth a damn"

- folk song with unknown origins.

Prologue

When I left UTC and went to Flagler College, I thought the creative writing workshops were going to be better. I was wrong.

As professors piled needless (and often wrong) praise upon me I started to feel something like *injustice*.

During my Senior year, my creative writing teacher invited the class to his house. We were invited to read anything we wanted.

We sat in a big circle. I think there were nineteen people there, including the teacher.

I read "In Which Language Do I Keep Silent" by Earl Braggs.

By the time I got to "what it's like to have nothing...but..."

I teared up. I didn't want to but on the other hand, I *thought* I was delivering with all the drama.

By the time I got to "Some mornings, I know my dreams lie" I choked up.

I had to stop.

Get your shit together I thought.

I did.

When I finished I looked up for the first time. Everyone had tears running down their faces.

Thank goodness "The Earl of Everything" had not been published yet.

What a massacre that would have been.

Mr. Braggs, no one can write like you.

"The rain knows more than the rain," you said.

I'm not sure if your favorite English word is velocity or rain. But I think it is rain.

I write for you and the rain.

Table of Contents

I.

Movements

I don't understand

the south

this state

this country

Black Lives Matter is moving

with beautiful poetry

I wear a "Make Racism Wrong Again"

t-shirt to my local gym

All these white people

leer at me

FUCK. YOU.

I think

over

and

over

I hit the black and blue weights even harder

headphones on

Zack de la Rocha screaming in my ears

I stare down anyone who

even

looks in my direction

Adrenaline rising like fires burning trees in California

I want to hurt someone

so

badly.

Out On Chickamauga Lake Looking For My Youth

I pull the oars back,
sweeping onto the green lake,
feeling the smoothness of the water
flow into my arms and body.
Out across from me a red mud island
kneels like a soldier over a fallen comrade.

The afternoon sun flashes
off the water onto the gray cliffs
dancing above the lake,
like a dare you can't refuse
a place where local kids
can feel a blinding crimson fall
to remind them of life.

I want the urge to dive
from those cliffs again
my eyes blurring,
the air rushing,
trying to keep me from
hitting that cold water.

But I'll sit here until
the house lights sparkle off
the water like glitter
on a sad girl's face
and remember a day when
the orange trees began
to fade to brown

and I yearned to feel that free.

I slip down into this
dirty, old dinghy watching

some kid in yellow shorts leap off
cheered on by his friends.

December 23 2019

all I can remember is rain

in
hard
dark
rain
Atlanta
traffic

I couldn't get to you fast enough

in
hard
dark
rain
Atlanta
traffic

your mom was threatening to kill herself

and you

your texts and calls

then silence

in
hard
dark
rain
Atlanta
traffic

I finally made it

you were on the apartment porch
in boxers
with two little boxes
and your little black dog

I grabbed you and put you

into

a warm car
with your dog
and your boxes

we drove home

to safety

listening to classic Christmas music

until then I thought you were dead

in
hard
dark
rain
Atlanta
traffic

Glass Vases

you built your heaven and called it hell
only wanting to possess the flowers
your father threw at your mother
spattering the green glass vase
all over the walls.

wide-eyed and sad you dipped
your fingers in the cool water
every Sunday morning
touching your lips,
praying for a kiss of freedom.

alone in your room you stared at crisp daisies
plucked fresh from a field no one could see.
yellow tears on a dirty pillow
your black widow cobweb dreams at night
for this life you might want someday.

go ahead, smash the vase against
the floor with your father's hand,
grab a bright green shard
and spill your mother's blood onto the floor.

A Conversation With Geese

I sat by the lake while the sky
darkened its blue

taking everything with it.

The geese approached, whispering
in their buzzing voices
floating on the air like piano wire.

I sat and looked at the island
of trees out across from me
and remembered all the nights

of my faded youth
spent

under this deepening Tennessee sky,
all the boats I've seen on the this lake
their green and red lights
bouncing off the stars.

I thought of the girls I've shared
the orange and pink sunsets with,
how this blue filled their eyes.
They're long gone now.

Off in the distance

a single boat
sends little ripples toward the shore
wrinkling the flat water.

I look up and see the geese
have left me – floating away

their black heads held high,
murmuring words
I do not understand.

Crown the River Prince

"What I seek...I cannot find"

- William Wordsworth

The naked red mud of the Tennessee river
floats across from me as
the smell of decay fills my mind.
I was the prince here, long ago,
my kingdom much smaller,
everything within my grasp.

The trees protected
the cloudy pools of rainwater
and my throne of an old trunk.
Now the pools are sad and tired,
as if weary of reflecting the sky.

Today, I danced on a picnic table
hearing the echoes of birds
who lived in my kingdom.
And the fallen oaks who once
served as my advisors settled
deeper into the ground.

A rusted barrel sits behind me
sinking into the Chattanooga mud
and the empty branches shake ghosts
from one to another
pointing the way home.

The fields sigh...

To calm myself

from isolation

I would get in my car and turn left

heading for curvy roads
and drive as fast as I could

on the final stretch of three miles I would hit 140 mph
at least

I saw him standing there
frozen with his antlers
brown
and
white
and
magnificent

at the last second he saw death

and as I plowed into him

I saw

it too

A Couple Weekends Ago In Key West

For Kat

The collapse of tequila
sinks into my legs
as we step off the street
into a dimly lit store dancing
with the light of clear crystals.
We step through the room,
your glittering and glowing lips
murmuring some song.

The glass candles offer escape,
a crystal vision of an empty future,
primary colors fading into
the shelves full of paintings and glassware.

Out on the street,
littered with pink and blue people,
the crowds speak against
the music and cool breeze.
We walk through the night,
silent in our private prayers,
whispering Smashing Pumpkins lyrics.

Forgetting How To Listen

"But two weeks later he killed her. Of course."

- Mike
- "Half Measures." Breaking Bad, created by Vince Gilligan, season 3, episode 12, Sony Pictures Television, 2010.

You have to go
    but he can be sweet

You have to go
    but I don't want him to be alone

You have to go
    but sometimes he doesn't hit me

You have to go
    but he brings me flowers

You have to go
    but he owns so many guns

You have to go
    but he cut back on his drinking

You have to go
    but you won't

until you're gone.

A Wrinkled Lady

I felt like a drop of water
dripping into a fountain
falling down with a lack of gravity
as some palm-reading card shark told
my fortune with some dingy blue cards,
in her dusty trailer full of
dying orange sunlight and dust.

She found life in the palm of my hand

I couldn't see truth in her eyes.

She smiled a lot with her wrinkled brow,
trying too hard to find a path into my thoughts

too many questions about love and love lost
like fireflies trying to find one another
among the night trees
green and yellow.

I wonder if she can see beyond
those metal walls.

I trembled slightly feeling her cool finger
on my palm and tried to gather
the strength to leave.

I walked out into the cool dusk breeze
leaving behind me the smoky air
and her beliefs in my future.

Asleep

remember when the days never seemed to end

and we were happy to see the fireflies?

and now we dread the sight of the stars

because another day has left us in this

life racing away and we can never catch

up to it again.

II.

"The truth is always an abyss."

- Franz Kafka

Capturing the Moon

I would park under a green sign
and walk
down
your street.

big grey shades
covering your
picture window

you moved
in shadow.

dancing to Tori Amos
I would hear your voice
above your stereo.

in the cool evening
sky

I brought you the moon
and begged her
to have mercy
on this cold rock

heavy
in my arms.

Walking Out of South Carolina

it's a green summer day
the cloud shocking blue
cloudless for now

these desolate roads
packed with
old trailers
and older houses
most of them brown

so many Goodwill stores
and white stores
selling jesus
yellow Dollar Generals
and so many signs for god

I can't rely
on your feelings
anymore

they change
so often
day
to
day

the day darkens
and it begins to rain
grey
and
cold

from beaches far away
it pours

in waves
down my face

I can't tell
if

you
are crying.

Concrete

scream your tears

a broken wine glass falling
to the floor of your shallow

scream at me those words

envy and greed for broken dreams
and this little girl who watched
fairies dance among the trees
growing in your father's backyard

your mother lived in a concrete world
and the floor was always cold
as if ghosts settled down there

to haunt your wanderings.

and you lay there letting them
fill your head with angels
who wanted to hang themselves
from your father's trees.

and as you stand in the orchard now,
do you really believe that
you are heavenly now?

and you must abandon your fragile wings
and join the angels you watched
die night after night?

The Gate

I got your painting yesterday
Packed tightly in its brown paper.
I imagined you, in your New York loft
desperately trying to paint sandy beaches.

I thought it was another of your abstractions,
with its smeared colors of green and black.

But as my eyes blurred
like falling asleep in front of a TV

I noticed gnarled dead trees
tangled with thorny vines
and an ancient iron gate
with a rusted heavy lock.

Far away
          beyond the gate
I saw a ray of sunlight shining
onto fresh blooming orchids.

I am outside the gate

          and there is no one to let me in.

the fireflies flew
over
us

bright yellow flashes

I almost felt
their tears
on
my
face.

Somewhere

in Tennessee
a man looks up at his IV
and says

fuck you Tennessee

a boy with blonde hair
and colored fingernails
is thrown into a river

fuck you Tennessee

at a private high school graduation
in Chattanooga
a boy is called a faggot

as he reaches out for his scroll

in 2024

fuck you Tennessee

fuck you Tennessee

fuck you Tennessee

The Circus

the ruins of my circus
lie in
broken shadows
of smoke

from the black tent

and elephants of ash

circling the ring

dusty trunks dragging the ground.

snow white clowns dance
cartwheels across from me.

I see
a dark violet-blue sky
through holes in the tent.

strange here in these wooden stands,
the acrid smell of despair
burns the air
like jasmine and cotton candy.

years ago, I laughed with the clowns
blind to their empty eyes
and hollow antics

and a ringmaster bent on travel

eyes away in the clouds.

I imagine you painted your lips red
to stand out against your white body

dancing toward me grey against
the yellow light of the carnival.

I blink my eyes and you are gone.

I slip into the mischief
of a boy who still believed in
the glory of the high wire

and the brave tiger leaping

through the flames

orange skin ablaze

of my life.

Silent Haven

Weather-beaten white wood, rough and splintering
from storms swept off the ocean.
I step inside where the door once was,
the house is musty, a thick smell
fills me from the rotting pews.

Walls once dark, now cracked and faded,
the building somehow holds together.
The stained glass of brilliant crimson and jade
are gone, except for one

with jesus raising his arms to heaven.

I see the podium still stands
behind it the choir loft looks down.
Outside the wind blows in dark clouds
with every puff
the building moans.

The rafters above, once polished oak,
look more like railroad ties now.

On one of them, a black bird has built a nest.

Heading outside, I smell the coming rain.

My Sometimes Friend

For Kat (again)

She calls herself my sometimes friend,
a glow-in-the-dark moon

a red cherry

plucked fresh from a jar.

We walk in the forest and look for
butterflies to add to her collection.

She likes the blue ones, flitting on
the green vines climbing the oaks.

She talks of loves that can't find her,
of princes that don't exist.
She climbs into my head
to watch the nerve fibers grow,
snapping the ones she doesn't like.

I sweep her down into the leaves
and we roll, filling our clothes
with the musty smells of autumn.

The world just a round
blue and green drop in her bucket.

But sometimes she goes far away,
her eyes glaze, and she sinks to
her knees and cries,
"I'm not your friend today.

Untitled

It was autumn cold that night,
I must've been about seven
the year my father had a heart attack.

I rode the elevator down
and down
from the 15th floor
holding my mom's hand.

Outside, I looked up at his hospital window,
and saw him waving down at us.
Mom froze and stared up,
and gently waved back.

It was years before I realized
why she was crying.

lightning bolt

dedicated to the writing workshop that told me I should only fall once

last night was like a hundred years

I fell
        and fell

watching myself in a small room
in the bed I slept in as a child
with the midnight blue of night
filling the room
and the lightning crashed and raged
as my statues of stone
smashed one another
just a few miles

        down the stairs...

For (Any) Reason

I don't know

or understand

history all that well

but I know

this country

this red and blue

divide

divide

divide

falling off a cliff

will end up back where it started

Jim Crow laws

written new again

you tell me you are a christian

I ask

Classic jesus

Or republican jesus?

In Nashville

late in 2020

we were drinking at a bar

with red and black walls

and as we walked through a protest

crowd

the cops circled

blue lights flashing

like
vultures

or piranha

I stopped

and stood
finger in the air

you won't shoot a white boy
but you **dam** sure are just looking

for any reason

to hurt the people around me

the air smelled like hope.

finally

I walked on

tears rolling down my face.

In A Kingdom By The Sea

White clouds with unending blue
dance through your body into
an infinity of feeling
like being of afraid of having
that nightmare where you
just keep falling...

Dreaming myself to sleep
I see your eyes last, before the dark.
There's a glassiness there now
a wonder at the miracles of the world
how you can be so high and so low
at the same time.

There are lines on your face now
that were smooth years ago
and under the eyes

scars
    for the things you have seen.

You come to me crying for release
from the hands in your head.
If only you could go back
to our dreams
    long ago.

We built our castles out of sand.
I guess my noble horse wasn't white enough
and your golden hair wasn't long enough
our castles melted into the sea

Flashes

(For Kat yet again)

That night drive,
up I-95
        3am

a red car and Smashing Pumpkins
        on repeat

those lonesome lyrics
        against
                each exit
a fleeting promise in the black night
        an opportunity for defeat.

we argued about whether
Pisces Iscariot was good

then you would pause all audio
        and read to me

short stories

the one about the guy dying
        on trial
                and choosing to drop into hell

has haunted me my whole life.

you were a blend of magic and freedom

a hue of purple defiance

against the monotony of the never-ending asphalt.

of suicide, depression, and anxiety

(for Tracey)

anxious
        a word
                I sometimes

forget
        how to spell.

Jupiter
        Florida
                the white beaches
                        (breaches)

you drove me
        to
                your secret spot.

down a sand road
        between
                bright
                        yellow and blue houses.

it was all
        purple dusk

we reached the sea
        blue
                in the dying light.

I started shaking

we walked
        down the sand
                tumbles between our toes.

a cool salt breeze
    huffed down the beach.

you looked
    at
        me.

your brown eyes
    into
        my blue.

I trembled
    and talked about
        insomnia.

you laughed

    welcoming me
        to the club.

far off

two clouds
    collided.

For Kat
(one last time)

"Por favor no fumar"
you would
sing
every time we stepped
onto an elevator

and giggle

your smile
white clouds
even on a blue day

remember calling me and telling me to get ready?
you pulled up in your car
wearing a t-shirt that said
"Shirley Manson is god"
and told me we were going to see Garbage

I said, who the fuck is Garbage?
You idiot, you said

remember driving to
South Beach?

you had just transformed
your hair purple

and as we slipped into Miami
the skyline
turned
purple with blue

clouds

over the MacArthur Causeway
we went
listening to Depeche Mode.

we didn’t need
a map

believe me

even
now.

The Night You Tried To Die

"I am not well; I could have built the Pyramids with the effort it takes me to cling on to life and reason."

- Franz Kafka, Letters to Felice

The night you tried to die
I didn't know what to do

The night you tried to die
You texted me and said goodbye

The night you tried to die
Something broke inside me

The night you tried to die
Time stood still

The night you tried to die
All I could do was panic

The night you tried to die
All I could do was drive fast

The night you tried to die
I would have followed you.

IV.

Failing With Magic

"They cannot fix you
they try and try..."

- Hummel, Maria, author. “House and Fire.”, by The American Poetry Review, 2003.

The arrogance
of this man in white
shining before me
in the grey light,
his confidence never seems to fade
even as I do.

The slow parade
of sleights of hand
they do nothing...

I cannot blink,
I see the other hand moving,
the deceit,
as he fools himself
into thinking he can fix me.

He hands me new white pills,
        swallow these...

But they dry my mouth

        like the body of Christ on Sunday.

Bare

Staring up at the IV bags
I try to feel the drugs
mixing with my blood
does anything help?

Every day
you
put your fingers
around my wrist

and you smile
bright and hollow

But I know
what you are doing
feeling me get smaller,
wasting away,
checking the progress

Do my wrist bones
dig into your fingertips
more than yesterday?

Is it fast enough for you?

I turn over
and feel my hip bone
dig into the mattress.

Smiling, I close my eyes
and fall into the dark.

And Again

"It was then I prayed, pleading with heaven."

- Hummel, Maria, author. “House and Fire.”, by The American Poetry Review, 2003.

For the hundredth
thousandth
time
I've lost count
the sickness returns

No more
not this time
        please

And the words come
sliding off my lips
mumbling
to a stone deaf god

I give up

Please, let me go
just

please
        please
                please

Haunted on Morphine

I wonder if the mattress
in this bed
is made of wood
and where will it go
when I am gone?

who will lie here next?

and these tubes
pouring forth from my arms
the bubbles slowly descend
and I think of my blood
and you

the silence of your ghosts
enter into me
and I cannot shake them.

A walk

It is not fun
to stumble down a hospital hallway
hanging onto your IV pole.

It is on wheels and full of bags

bags of magic that don't do anything

But you go
step by step
toward the window at the end
blue sky and red leaves

just to turn back
for a dark room
another pill
and another injection

then the dark.

The hospital corridor

The machines beep.

At 3am
lights are bright
they look as if they have a green tint.

I unhook my machines
and wander out of my room

scanning and computer equipment line the hall.

No one else around
I just wander.

empty it feels
but full of sleeping people.

I think of going outside
I could pull it off

Maybe.

I walk down to the ER
and see a gunshot victim
in emergency help
blood everywhere
"Just stop the bleeding"

I wish.

In another ER stall
UV lights pulse off the walls

disinfecting it from something
horrible.

The waiting room is crowded
with people who need help.

Help.

I go back to my room
and crawl into cold sheets.

Always the lights
they will be in soon for my blood
more and more and more
it never ends.

The machines beep.

Epilogue

"I am a dream catcher
who has simply
forgotten
how
to catch dreams."

- Braggs, Earl, author. "Crossing Tecumseh Street", by Anhinga Press, 2003.

"the opposite of silence
is silence"

- Bob-Waksberg, Raphael, author. "Someone Who Will Love You In All Your Damaged Glory", by Vintage Books, 2020.

"Faith, like a guillotine. As heavy, as light."

- Franz Kafka

Acknowledgments

This book would not have happened without the encouragement of my wife Amiee and my early readers and editors Anastasia Smith, Andrew Virdin, and Bryan Center. I love all of you.

Cover art by Anastasia Smith

About the Author

Chad Smith is a consultant and author hiding out in the Caribbean.

www.ingramcontent.com/pod-product-compliance
Lightning Source LLC
Chambersburg PA
CBHW072233190626
46809CB00017B/1904

9798895871034